Adh-3252

SANTA CRUZ CITY-COUNTY LIBRARY SYSTEM
0000119013852

D0646514

Apt 8/08

Nathan's Wish

A Story about Cerebral Palsy

Laurie Lears

Illustrated by Stacey Schuett

ALBERT WHITMAN & COMPANY

Morton Grove, Illinois

For Vijay and Aneesh,
with special thanks to Mitzi Eaton.

—L.L.

To Ian, with love.

—S.S.

Library of Congress Cataloging-in-Publication Data

Lears, Laurie.
Nathan's wish : a story about cerebral palsy / by Laurie Lears ;
illustrated by Stacey Schuett.
p. cm.
Summary: A boy with cerebral palsy helps out at a raptor rehabilitation center and is inspired himself
when an owl that cannot fly finds another purpose in life.
ISBN 0-8075-7101-6 (hardcover)
[1. Cerebral palsy—Fiction. 2. People with disabilities—Fiction. 3. Wildlife rescue—Fiction.
4. Orphaned animals—Fiction.] I. Schuett, Stacey, ill. II. Title.
PZ7.L46365Nat 2005 [Fic]—dc22 2004021298

Text copyright © 2005 by Laurie Lears. Illustrations copyright © 2005 by Stacey Schuett.
Published in 2005 by Albert Whitman & Company,
6340 Oakton Street, Morton Grove, Illinois 60053-2723.
Published simultaneously in Canada by Fitzhenry & Whiteside, Markham, Ontario.
All rights reserved. No part of this book may be reproduced or
transmitted in any form or by any means, electronic or mechanical, including photocopying, recording, or
by any information storage and retrieval system, without permission in writing from the publisher.
Printed in the United States of America.
10 9 8 7 6 5 4 3 2 1

For more information about Albert Whitman & Company,
visit our web site at www.albertwhitman.com.

About Cerebral Palsy

Cerebral palsy is caused by altered brain development before, during, or in the early months following birth. The injury is permanent and can occur from an infection, lack of oxygen, bleeding in the brain, complications of premature birth, or even a genetic condition.

As a result, children with CP experience a wide range of challenges. Cerebral palsy impairs movement—it can be mild and limited, affecting only part of the body, or it may be more significant, requiring a person to use crutches or a wheelchair. Cerebral palsy is sometimes complicated by other challenges such as hearing or vision problems, epilepsy, or learning disabilities. However, like Nathan, more than half of those with cerebral palsy have no impairment in their thinking or learning.

For a child like Nathan, the challenges are easily seen—he requires a wheelchair or a walker to move about and needs assistance with common daily activities. At times, he may feel passive and dependent on others, unsure that he has anything to contribute. Children in this situation risk becoming demoralized by a focus on their disabilities rather than their strengths and natural assets.

Resilience is an important human characteristic that can be nourished in children facing adversity. This can be achieved by mentoring or support by reliable adults, including parents, teachers, therapists, friends, and neighbors, and through frequent opportunities for the child to feel successful and needed. In this story, Nathan has the good fortune to discover all these things in an experience that fosters in him a sense of well-being and worth, while diminishing the disabling potential of cerebral palsy.

W. Carl Cooley, M.D., Medical Director
Crotched Mountain Rehabilitation Center
Greenfield, New Hampshire

My neighbor, Miss Sandy, is a Raptor Rehabilitator. That means she takes care of injured birds of prey, like owls and hawks, until they are well enough to fly again.

Every day I watch Miss Sandy mix medicines, give out food, and clean the big cages in her backyard. No matter how tired or busy she is, Miss Sandy always takes time to talk to me about the birds.

More than anything, I wish I could walk by myself. Then I would help Miss Sandy with her chores instead of just watching her. But I have cerebral palsy, and my muscles don't work well enough for me to get around without my wheelchair or walker.

One day Miss Sandy shows me a Screech Owl with a broken wing. Even though the owl's wing is set in a splint, she flaps against the sides of her crate, trying to escape.

"She'll have to stay here until her wing heals," says Miss Sandy. "What do you think we should call her, Nathan?"

The owl's bright yellow eyes flash with anger. "How about Fire?" I say.

"That's a good name for her," says Miss Sandy. "I hope Fire will calm down soon."

But day after day, Fire fights to be free, and I worry that she might hurt herself again.

At last Miss Sandy takes the splint off Fire's wing and moves her to a cage.

"Fire needs to practice using her wing a little at a time," she tells me.

As the weeks go by, Fire's wing grows stronger and she is moved to a bigger cage. Sometimes Fire ignores the dead mice that Miss Sandy puts into her cage and peers out at the sky instead. I can tell that Fire wants to go hunting for her own food. "How much longer will she have to stay?" I ask.

"A broken wing takes a long time to get strong again," says Miss Sandy. "I believe you are as impatient as Fire, Nathan!"

Miss Sandy is right. I can't wait for Fire to be free. When I see a bird flying outside the window at school, I think about Fire and forget to listen to what my teacher is saying.

At night I hear a ghostly cry coming from Miss Sandy's yard and wonder if Fire is calling to her friends.

One day Fire's cage is empty. She is inside a small box that Miss Sandy is holding in her hands. "I'm going to put Fire in the flight cage to see how far she can fly," Miss Sandy tells me.

My heart thumps in my ears as I follow along. Maybe if Fire flies well enough, Miss Sandy will let her go today!

I suck in my breath as Miss Sandy gently dumps Fire out of the box and into the huge flight cage.

Fire springs forward and soars through the air, looking strong and beautiful.

But suddenly she tilts to one side and begins to drop lower in the cage. Even though I squeeze my eyes closed, I hear a soft thud as Fire tumbles to the ground.

When I open my eyes, Miss Sandy is shaking her head. And all at once I realize that Fire can never be released. Her wing isn't strong enough for her to survive in the wild.

"Poor Fire," says Miss Sandy. "She wished so badly to be free."

I turn away so Miss Sandy won't see the tears slipping down my cheeks.

I know just how it feels to wish for something that can't come true.

After that, the light goes out of Fire's eyes. She refuses to eat and doesn't even try to escape from her cage. "Please don't give up, Fire," I whisper. But Fire sits as still as a statue on her perch.

There must be some way I can help Fire. I search on my computer for information about injured birds. I read about a Great Horned Owl who is nearly blind. She takes care of orphaned baby owls until they are old enough to be released.

Maybe Fire could do that, too! I print out the article and show it to Miss Sandy. "It's worth a try," she says. "I have three nestlings who were orphaned in the storm last week."

Miss Sandy puts the nesting box in Fire's cage. The baby owls bob their heads and make funny peeping sounds. But Fire does not seem to care about the hungry nestlings, or anything else.

I cannot bear to see her looking so sad.

I stay at home feeling sorry for Fire—and myself.

One evening I hear a pounding at our door, and Miss Sandy comes rushing inside. "Come with me, Nathan!" she cries. "You must see Fire!"

Before I know what is happening, I am bumping along the path to Miss Sandy's house.

Miss Sandy parks me outside of Fire's cage. "Look!" she whispers.

I can hardly believe my eyes! Fire picks up a piece of meat from the ground, hops up to the nesting box, and stuffs the meat into a baby owl's mouth.

Although Fire's wish to be free can't come true, she has found something important to do. And that gives me an idea!

The next day I go to Miss Sandy's house and look around her yard. I may not be able to walk by myself, but I am going to find a way to help Miss Sandy with her chores.

I know the buckets are too heavy for me to carry, yet maybe I can fill the birds' bathing basins with the hose. It takes a long time to untangle the hose and drag it to each cage. But I don't give up until all the basins are full.

When I see the mail truck coming down the road, I hurry to the end of the driveway and wait for the mail carrier to give me Miss Sandy's mail. I tuck the letters into my jacket pocket and take them inside.

When it's time for Miss Sandy to feed the birds, I offer to stay in the office and answer the phone for her. The phone rings four times, and I carefully write down every message.

Before I leave for home, Miss Sandy reaches out and hugs me. "You were a big help to me today, Nathan," she says.

I duck my head and my cheeks burn. But I cannot keep from smiling. Now I know just how proud Fire must feel!